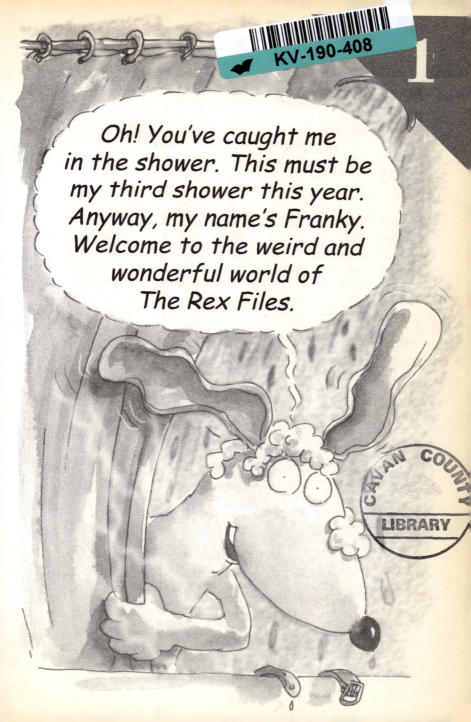

Rex is my boss.
I can't imagine
him taking a
shower. Nothing
itchy would dare
live on him.
He'd soon sort
them out.

Together, we've solved many
mysteries. You may have read or
heard about some of our cases.

ZIP!

There was the
extraordinary case
of The Bermuda
Triangle. Flies kept
disappearing.
Rex nearly gave up
on the case, but he
solved it with a
flash of inspiration.

There was also
the case of Lilly
La More, the
Vampire Vixen.
There was
nothing
mysterious about
the way Rex fell
for her charms,
but we won't talk
about that here.

Rex says that anything mysterious or
paranormal is usually a trick.

Frankly, Franky,
anything strange is just
hanky-panky!

One of the most difficult things we come across are bugs and viruses. They're so difficult to see and they're so busy changing and mutating that you never know what they are going to do next.
And they can give you all sorts of illnesses and allergies.

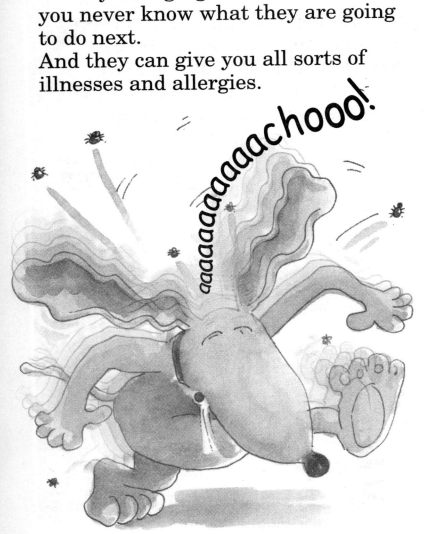

aaaaaaaaaaaachooo!

Anyway, let me tell you about the strange case of The Shredder.

Sometimes Rex knows when there is a new case coming up. He can spot the signs. One day, while I was itching and sneezing like mad, Rex was busy reading the paper…

aaaaaaaaaachooo!

For goodness sake, use your hanky, Franky.

The Terrier

Mystery Illness hits Snake Community

Mr. Asprey Slipwinder
makes a speech

Leaders of the snake community met yesterday to decide what can be done about the mystery illness known as *Soft Shed Syndrome.* **Sufferers shed their skin as normal, but have no new skin to replace it.**

They are left to end their days in small, dark, damp places, rejected by their friends who fear that they may catch the disease too.

A recent sufferer of S.S.S.

Later that afternoon
I was doing a bit of filing, when
someone started knocking on
our door.

I opened the door, but there was nobody there. I looked down the street. It was deserted. Then a small voice hissed in my ear.

The snake came in and introduced himself as Thymon.

Thymon curled up under Rex's desk lamp and told us his story.

You may have read about thith thnake illneth called thoft thed thyndrome? It'th thumtimeth called eth eth eth for thort. Well, I think I'm going to get it thoon, but I don't think it'th really an illneth.

Excuthe me, my name's not Thymon. It's Thimon with an eth. You know, eth for thnake.

Well, Thymon, we have heard about SSS but I'd like to know why you think it isn't an illness.

Ah! SIMON!

As Simon was speaking, I couldn't stop looking at his eyes. They made me feel so sleepy. Snakes can do that to you.

A couple of month ago, Uncle Tham went to thed hith thkin ath uthual. When he woke up, both hith new and hith old thkin were gone.

Rex thought we should go and
visit Simon's Uncle Sam.
We found him in a dark, jungly
sort of place. He was living under
a cold, slimy rock. It was a
horrible place. It made me want
to …

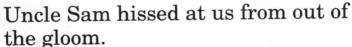
Uncle Sam hissed at us from out of the gloom.

I went for a test at the SSSSS. That's short for the Soft Shed Syndrome Sufferers' Society. They did some tests. They said I was very likely to get the disease. But I don't feel like I'm suffering from a disease. I feel like I've had my skin taken away from me.

A few days later, Rex saw
another article about
SSS in the paper.
To be honest, one more snake
getting a rare disease is not
much of a story, so it was only
a small article on page 9.

May 19th   Page 9

Latest Case of SSS

A new case of Soft
Shed Syndrome or SSS
was reported by the
SSSSS (Soft Shed
Syndrome Sufferers'
Society) this week.
Mr Asprey Slipwinder,
President of the SSSSS,
said that "the patient
wishes to remain
anonymous".

*Asprey Slipwinder
yesterday*

Condemned to live in
darkness by SSS.

6 Rex has contacts everywhere. An old friend from his college days worked on a newspaper. He gave Rex some background information on the SSSSS and their telephone number. But, of course, he wanted *all* the details if we uncovered a story! Rex phoned up the SSSSS and made an appointment to meet them.

We didn't recognise Asprey Slipwinder until he introduced himself.

You look different from your picture in the papers, Mr Slipwinder.

Ha ha ha! I'm not very photogenic, y'know? This is my colleague Doctor Sssarenson. He's looking for a DNA marker to prove that SSS is a genetic complaint passed down through families.

What piercing eyes he has!

We keep hearing stories about the Shredder. Do you think there's any truth in them?

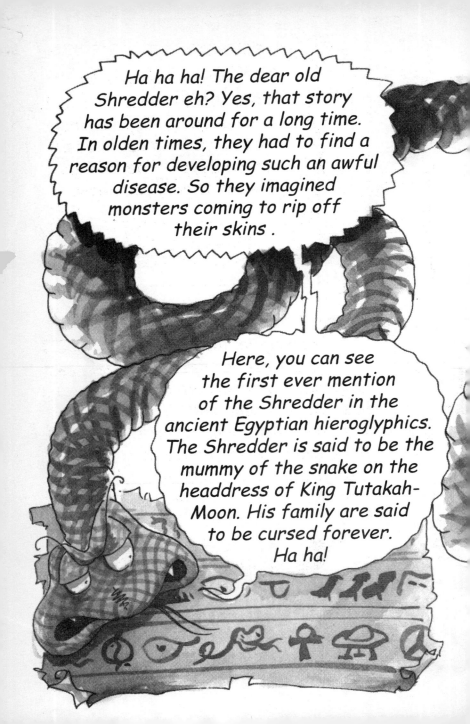

Here it is again, in the Viking runes. It's a story about a serpent from the south. This could easily mean Egypt. The Vikings went there, you know.

Then again, in the Dark Ages, the Shredder was feared. But these were simple folk. They didn't have the science that we have today. With time and patience, the SSSSS will solve this problem once and for all.

S'hreddivs Aspá terrifia

Rex was very interested in the history of the Shredder.

If the history of the Shredder goes all the way back to ancient Egypt, I think we should go and do a little research in the museum.

Good idea. I've always wanted to see the mummy of King Tutakah-Moon.

MUSEUM

The mummy and the fabulous, gold death mask of King Tutakah-Moon was very impressive.

The Mummy and Death Mask of King Tutakah-Moon. 3000 BC.

The headdress is made from 22 carat gold. The snake motif is of an asp or Egyptian Viper. It was the poison from an asp's bite that killed Queen Cleopatra.

I got myself a souvenir guide book

All that talk about shedding skins made me feel itchier than ever! When I got home that night I made straight for the shower.

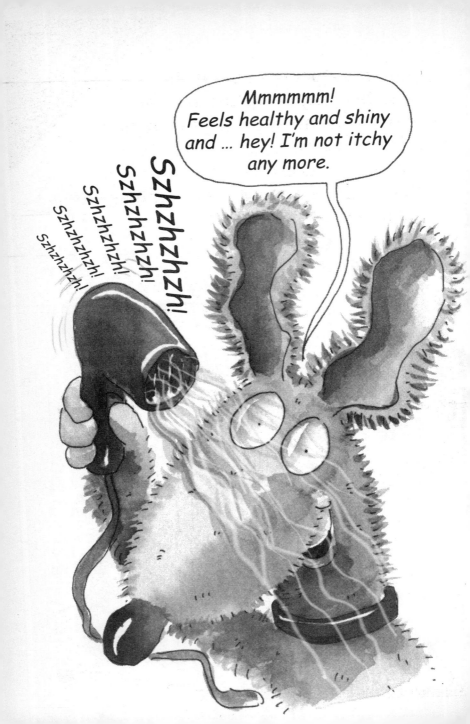

Simon helped us spend the
next few days reading books
about ancient Egypt. We learned
a lot of interesting things about
mummies and pharaohs and asps.
Reading the newspaper came as
light relief.

When I was at school, my teacher thought I would be a librarian when I grew up. I think it's because I like things to be all tidy and in their place. Anyway, I quickly found a collection of useful newspaper cuttings from my filing system. They all had pictures of Asprey on them. We spread them out on the table and examined them.

Incredible!

Amazing!

!

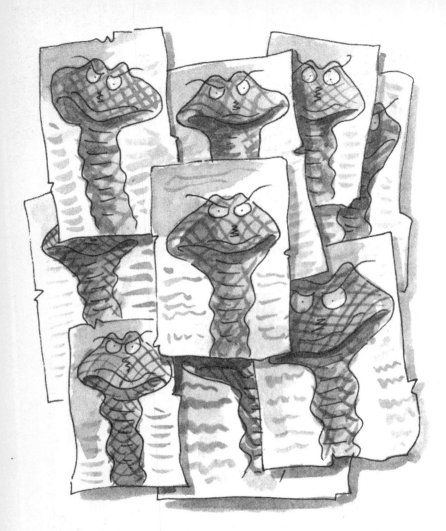

None of the pictures of Asprey
Slipwinder was the same. You could
tell it was him, but his skin pattern
was different in every picture. It was
like a spot-the-difference competition.

With the newspaper clippings was a form to fill in and send to the SSSSS.

Soft Shed Syndrome Sufferers-Society
Are You Worried?
Does your skin pattern look like this?

If it does, draw your pattern in the grid below and send it to **SSSSS**
PO BOX 43, Adderly.

Name ....
Address ....
....
....

Franky, I sense hanky-panky!

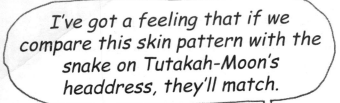

The next day, Simon phoned to tell us that the SSSSS had been in touch and wanted to do some tests.

Simon came as soon as he could and told us what sort of tests the SSSSS had done on him.

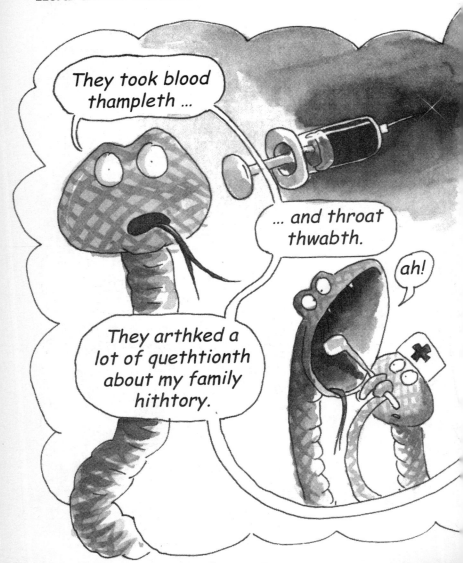

10

Rex always says that if we are to help different animals we have to try to think like them. Actually, to tell you the truth, I'm usually terrified of snakes, so I've not given them much thought.

It's this shedding business I find hard to understand. It's like snakes are trying to live forever. When we get to look old and tired, that's tough! But snakes get a fresh new skin and start all over again.

Snakes don't live forever, do they?

Now that I'd stopped itching and sneezing, I found I could think clearly again. Unlike poor Simon. He was starting to go into skin-shedding mode.

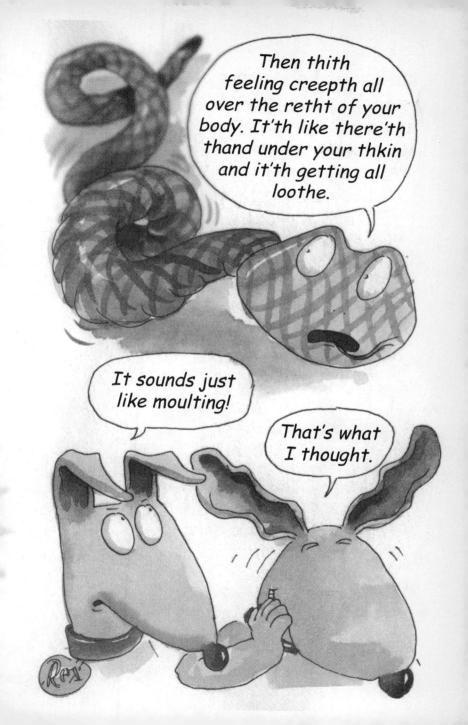

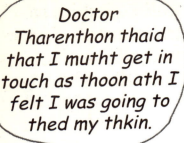

Rex found a towel and rolled it up. He held it together with coloured elastic bands. He put two red stickers on the front and it looked just like a snake ... well, sort of.

After hunting through the storeroom in the office, we found three small mirrors, then we went round to Simon's. He showed us where he went to shed his skin. It was a large rock.

Simon helped to ease the towel snake
into the space underneath the rock.
Rex peered in to have a look.

Rex gave us each a little mirror.

11

We found a perfect place to
hide. By using our mirrors
we could see the rock entrance
very clearly.

*I thpy with my
little eye, thumthing
beginning with Eth.*

"S"?

We waited and we watched. We
watched and we waited. When you
watch detectives on the TV,
you don't see this part of the job!
Soon after darkness had fallen,
something slithered by.

It entered Simon's shedding place.
There was a lot of hissing.

SSSSSSSSSSSSS!

There was a lot of cursing too.

Rex whispered to Simon and me to
keep looking in the mirrors.
Then he spoke out loud.

Asprey Slipwinder,
Come out.
I know it's you.

The extraordinary shape of a
mummified snake swayed in
front of us.

I am the Shredder!
Look deep into my eyes.

Your hypnotic
powers won't work
on us, Asprey.
We've got mirrors,
unlike your
victims.

12

The Shredder stopped swaying.

There is no Shredder.
I know it's you under
those bandages, Asprey.

Creating a double
bluff was very clever,
Asprey. You pretended to be
the Shredder, to keep that story
going and at the same time, you
started the SSSSS to make
snakes think that there really
is an illness.

They trusted
you and came to
you for help.

Then his skin came loose and tore itself into shreds, before it fell away.

It was hideous. Soon, he was nothing
but a skeleton.
Age had finally caught up with
Asprey Slipwinder.
He collapsed to the floor. The breath
went out of him.

Goodbye,
cruel
world.

13 Poor Doctor Sssarenson was most apologetic. Mind you, He had said that the Shredder was the most likely explanation for SSS. In a way he was right after all! It turned out that Asprey was actually related to King Tutakah-Moon's asp. His family had suffered from shredding, or what we now call SSS throughout the centuries.

So, maybe it was the Pharaoh's Curse after all?

Humph! That's hanky-panky, Franky!

Thymon, sorry, I mean Simon, came round to show us his new skin.

Like it?

Yes, very smart.
Next time you feel that
itch coming on, why don't you
try Head and Whiskers™?
Try it for two weeks,
It did wonders for me!

Order Form

THE REX FILES BOOKS ARE:

0 340 71432 8   The Life Snatcher
0 340 71466 2   The Phantom Bantam
0 340 71467 0   The Bermuda Triangle
0 340 71468 9   The Shredder
0 340 71469 7   The Frightened Forest
0 340 71470 0   The Baa-Baa Club

If you enjoyed this book you may want to read more about Rex and Franky, or other books by Shoo Rayner, like *The Ginger Ninja*, a wonderful series of books about a young cat called Ginger.

Ginger is a happy kitten.
He likes all his school friends,
loves playing pawball,
and even enjoys his lessons!
Until Tiddles comes to St Felix's . . .
When Tiddles joins the class,
it's soon clear he may be the
biggest bully the school
has ever known . . .

If you would like to read more about Ginger
(and find out how he becomes best friends with Tiddles),
the Ginger Ninja books are available at your local bookshop
or newsagent, or may be ordered direct from the publisher.

Phone 01235 400414 and have your credit card ready.

0 340 61955 4   The Ginger Ninja
0 340 61956 2   The Return of Tiddles
0 340 61957 0   The Dance of the Apple Dumplings
0 340 61958 9   St Felix for the Cup
0 340 69379 7   World Cup Winners
0 340 69380 0   Three's a Crowd

Please allow the following for postage and packing:
UK & BFPO – £1.00 for the first book, 50p for the second book, and 30p for each additional book ordered up to a maximum charge of £3.00.

OVERSEAS & EIRE – £2.00 for the first book, £1.00 for the second book, and 50p for each additional book.

First published in Great Britain in 1999
by Hodder Children's Books

Copyright © 1999 Shoo Rayner

The right of Shoo Rayner to be identified as the Author of the Work has been
asserted by him in accordance with the
Copyright, Designs and Patents Act 1988

ISBN 0 340 71468 9

10   9   8   7   6   5   4   3   2   1

A Catalogue record for this book is available from the British Library

Printed and bound by
The Guernsey Press Co. Ltd. Guernsey, Channel Islands

For
Andy & Caroline

Meet Rex and Franky
on the Internet!
www.shoo-rayner.co.uk

*Hodder
Children's
Books*